In memory of Nana and Pop
—C.F.

To Ellie and Bethany with love
—R.T.

This edition produced 2004 for
BOOKS ARE FUN LTD
1680 Hwy 1 North, Fairfield, IA 52556

by LITTLE TIGER PRESS
An imprint of Magi Publications
1 The Coda Centre, 189 Munster Road, London SW6 6AW
www.littletigerpress.com

First published in the United States 2003 by
Harry N. Abrams, Incorporated, New York
100 Fifth Avenue, New York, NY 10011
Abrams is a subsidiary of La Martinière Groupe

Originally published in Great Britain 2003
by Little Tiger Press, London

Text copyright © Claire Freedman 2003
Illustrations copyright © Rory Tyger 2003

ISBN 1 84506 113 6

Printed in China

2 4 6 8 10 9 7 5 3 1

Good Night, Sleep Tight

by

Claire Freedman

illustrated by

Rory Tyger

LITTLE TIGER PRESS

One night, Grandma was baby-sitting Archie.

"Aren't you sleepy yet, Archie?" asked Grandma.

"No!" replied Archie. "I don't feel sleepy at all. I'm wide awake!"

Grandma sat down on the edge of Archie's bed. "Have you got all your favorite friends to snuggle up with?" she asked. "They might help you feel sleepy."

"I've got Tiger and Rabbit," said Archie. "But where's Elephant?"

"Here he is," said Grandma, tucking Elephant in nice and snug. "Hold him tight and soon you'll feel sleepy."

But neither Archie nor his little friends went to sleep. "We're still wide awake, Grandma," he said.

"What about some nice warm milk?" said Grandma. "That makes me feel ready for bed."

Archie drank every
drop of his milk, but
he didn't feel sleepy.
"I'm still wide awake,
Grandma!" he said.
"Please can we watch
the fireflies? That
might make me
feel ready for
bed."

Grandma wrapped up Archie in his cozy blanket, and together they watched the dancing fireflies. Archie tried to count them, but it didn't make him feel tired. "I'm still wide awake, Grandma!" he said. "Would you sing me a lullaby, please? That might make me sleepy."

Grandma sang some of Archie's favorite songs. Archie closed his eyes and listened . . . but he didn't feel sleepy. "I'm still wide awake, Grandma," he whispered.

"I know, Archie," Grandma said. "Let me rock you in my arms. That will make you sleepy."

Grandma rocked Archie
gently in her arms, all the way
down to the apple grove and
back. Archie felt safe and
warm in Grandma's arms, but
he didn't feel the tiniest
bit sleepy.

"Grandma, I'm STILL wide
awake!" he said. "Will you tell
me a story, please?
Listening to stories
makes me feel sleepy."

Grandma sat down comfortably,
and Archie snuggled up close
to her.

She told him stories about all the naughty things his mommy had done when she was as little as he was.

"Your mommy never felt sleepy at bedtime either," Grandma said.

Grandma carried Archie back inside. She smiled a secret smile as she remembered putting Archie's mommy to bed when she was little.

Grandma tucked
Archie into bed. She
pulled the covers right up to
his nose.

"I used to tuck your mommy
into bed, with the blankets pulled
right up to her nose—like this!"
said Grandma.

"Then I'd
stroke the top
of Mommy's
forehead—
like this,"
Grandma said.
   Very gently she
stroked the top of
Archie's forehead.

"And I'd give Mommy a very special good-night kiss,"
said Grandma.

Grandma gave
Archie a special
good-night kiss.

"That's right, Grandma," said Archie with a big yawn. "And then she says, 'Good night, sleep tight!'"

"That's right, Archie," said Grandma . . .

And before Grandma could even
say "Good night, sleep tight,"
Archie was fast asleep!